Fergus's Secret

For Tim

First published in 2005 in Great Britain by
Piccadilly Press Ltd, London
www.piccadillypress.co.uk

Text and illustrations copyright © Tony Maddox 2005

This 2010 edition published by Sandy Creek by arrangement with Piccadilly Press

Sandy Creek
122 Fifth Avenue
New York, NY 10011

ISBN: 978 1 4351 2332 8

1 3 5 7 9 10 8 6 4 2

Printed and bound in China

Fergus's
Secret

Tony Maddox

When Farmer Bob's
tractor broke down,
the animals did their
best to help around
the farm . . .

. . . but without the tractor they found the work
very tiring. After a few days the animals decided that
something had to be done!

They needed to earn some money to get the tractor repaired . . . but how?

After much discussion they came up with a plan . . .
a secret plan that Farmer Bob couldn't find out about
and that would depend on Fergus.

A few days later, the animals crept
quietly out of the farmyard leaving
Fergus behind on his own.

Shortly afterwards, Farmer Bob noticed how
quiet and empty the farmyard had become.
He decided he had better check on the animals.

He called into the barn.
"How are you today,
Mrs. Cow?"

Fergus called back,
"*MOOO!*"

"Good," said Farmer Bob as he
went off to check the pigs.
Fergus had to get there
before him.
The only way was across
the muddy yard.

When Farmer Bob called across to the pig shed, "How are my pigs today?" a very muddy Fergus answered, "*Oink, oink!*"

Oink Oink!

"Good," said Farmer Bob as he made his way over to the hens.

Fergus managed to
reach the henhouse
just in time.

When Farmer Bob called, "How are my ladies today?"
Fergus gasped, "*Quack, quack!*" OOOPS!

"Good," said Farmer Bob as he
set off towards the duck pond.
Suddenly he stopped.
"Hmm . . ." he said,
"hens don't go *quack,
quack*. They go
cluck, cluck."

Farmer Bob went back and peered through the henhouse window. He saw Fergus covered in mud, looking very sorry for himself.

"Fergus!" he cried, "What are you up to?" Fergus gave a long sigh. Now Farmer Bob would find out what the secret was.

But first Fergus needed to get cleaned up.

He led Farmer Bob to
the village.
The Summer Fair was
in full swing and
Farmer Bob was
about to have a few
surprises.

"My ducks!"
he gasped.

"My hens!"

He couldn't believe
his eyes when he saw
The World's Tallest Man.

"My pigs!" he cried.

But the biggest
surprise was yet
to come because
when he peeped
into the Fortune
Teller's tent, it
wasn't Madame
Clara he saw,
it was . . .

Mrs. Cow!

There in Mrs. Cow's crystal ball,
he saw his tractor, all repaired and
looking as good as new.

And guess what . . . ?

The crystal ball was absolutely right!
The animals had made enough money
to have the tractor repaired,
and everything on the farm
returned to normal.